EMILIANO FORINO PROCACCI

Sneak preview:
The Superhero of Emotion

Unstatus Luxury™
www.unstatusluxury.com

ISBN 979-8-218-00940-3

Illustrations by Cecilia Flumian

First Published in 2022

Introduction

Emiliano Forino Procacci is a psychotherapist specialized in facial micro-expressions and body language. He has created a new superhero, called Dr. Emotion, whose special power is to control the emotions of others.

His powers are very specific, based on real scientific studies,[1] as explained briefly below.

There are seven basic emotions: anger, fear, happiness, sadness, disgust, surprise, and contempt. Our faces can express each of these, including through facial micro-expressions.

Dr. Emotion's superhero power is that he can control the emotional state of others with his hands. Each movement of the fingers is linked to a specific emotion. Pushing a finger forward, the emotion in the person before him increases in intensity while by pulling back the finger, the emotion is reduced. In the novel, Oscar Path (Dr. Emotion's real name) struggles to remember which finger corresponds to which emotion, such as anger on the little finger and fear on the index finger, but after training at length, he manages to do so.

He gets his powers from three sources: an ancient red stone sewn into his suit, a machine invented by his father called Garbmel Life, and his genetics.

The complete story of Dr. Emotion has already been published in a book in Italian and will soon be available in English as well. This is a summary of the book's contents, illustrated with drawings.

---

[1] Ekman P., *Emotions revealed*, Holt Paperbacks, 2007.

PART 1

The suit fit his body like a glove, highlighting his muscles, and the pads on the shoulders and forearms gave it a formidable look that made it look like armor. It was turquoise and the chest bore the insignia of the Dedion — a downward-pointing metal sword on a gilt disc covered with gears decorated with lily and rose flowers.

That symbol was created by Oscar's father, inspired by forms he termed "archetypal." The sword pointing downwards was the emblem of the war, and given the resemblance to a cross, it was also a symbol of all the religions of humanity, from the oldest to the newest.

The gear wheels in the symbol referred to technological progress, to which Oscar's father had dedicated his life. He believed that the survival of the same human species over the millennia had been possible thanks to great scientific inventions such as the wheel. The decorations with lily flowers, on the other hand, represented the clarity of mind that should guide the scientist in his works, while the roses represented feminine purity and the infinite. Finally, the meaning attributed by Oscar's father to the golden disc referred to the scientist's aim which was not only to discover something new but also to proceed on a path that could lead him towards a process of inner enlightenment.

The suit gave no power to the wearer but was made of a special material made of mobile molecules that could adapt to environmental stimuli. In practice, if it was hit by the blade of a knife instead of resisting and tearing, it shaped to the knife point and made it slip away. The same was true of bullets or any other object.

PART 2

The new parents decided to name their son Oscar. As the father's last name was Path and he loved plays on words, he suggested they give the newborn baby this name — Oscar. The last name Path and the first two letters of the son's name "Os" create the Greek word "pathos" which means "to feel emotion."

As an adult, Oscar acquired his powers. One day he was walking quickly through the alleys of the historic center of Rome going home. The light from the streetlamps passing through a light blanket of fog lit his deep green eyes. His cloak, much like a cape, opened with each gust of wind to reveal a tight-fitting turquoise suit, with a symbol on the chest featuring a shiny red stone. Anyone would have thought Oscar's clothing strange, but he didn't care because he had just come back from an incredible adventure and humanity was in his debt.

Right then he came across a young couple who was arguing.

"So, you admit it? You fell in love with someone else?" the young man said loudly.

"If I fell in love with someone else, it's because you lied to me endless times!" she shouted, making a gesture with her hand to keep him at a distance.

Oscar stopped to observe the couple, then politely said, "Would you accept a piece of advice from a stranger?"

"Go away! We have enough problems as it is," the man replied, rolling up the sleeves of his jacket, ready to fight.

Oscar made a gesture with his hand from right to left as if he were turning the page of an invisible book hanging in the air, then he pulled back his little finger and pushed his thumb forward. The couple calmed down in an instant thanks to the stranger who had eased their anger. For a moment around them time seemed to slow down, even the raindrops began to float, interrupting their light dance. A careful eye would not have missed the physical changes that happened in the young couple. The muscles of their forehead were no longer contracted, and their pupils had changed size. The couple looked around in amazement, wondering what had happened. In that pause pregnant with expectation, Oscar stroked his short black hair with one hand and shook his head, smiling. "Anger consumes the body and the mind and sometimes some advice from a stranger can help," he whispered a moment before starting to walk again, leaving behind the young couple who were now embracing.

What was Oscar able to do? What exceptional power did he have? To understand what extraordinary events had happened in his life, we must take a step back and tell the story of what happened.

PART 3

Ancient peoples used to build temples on sacred ground to officiate important religious ceremonies and to gather in prayer. After blessing the area, a priest placed the first stone tracing a circular groove around it. The sacred symbol of the circle was made on the ground with a dot in the center, an emblem of the sun, gold and the individual ego. Once the building was completed, it was the high priest who placed inside it a relic to which extraordinary powers were given, a seal of the place's inviolability.

When the Erechtheion was founded, a high priest placed a large red stone in the center. According to legend, this object was created by the gods before there was life on earth. Later Zeus, realizing how fragile human beings were, decided to give them the stone by instilling immense power in it. One of its traits was to confuse the emotions of anyone who approached it, turning happiness into sadness, anger into joy and contempt into compassion.

One day the Erechtheion was sacked, the high priest lost his life, and the stone was stolen and taken away. Over time the precious object passed from hand to hand and from place to place until it reached Delphi in the Temple of Apollo, where the priestess Pythia gave those who asked predictions about future events. It was in that temple that the red stone took the name of Omphalos — the center of the earth — also called "the navel of the world." According to tradition, Pythia ordered the burning of bay leaves and barley flour, then she went to the sacred room located under the floor of the temple where the red stone was kept. In a room full of water vapor coming from a crack in the rock, the priestess, dipping laurel branches in a cauldron, performed the ritual to see into the future.

The temple of Apollo was plundered by the Gauls and the red stone disappeared for a long time until modern times, it was found in a dusty bazaar in a Turkish city and bought by a mysterious man with conspicuous scars on his arms and head. The stone was taken to a villa on the outskirts of Rome and placed inside a machine called Polemos which, according to unconfirmed rumors, could influence the emotions of human beings.

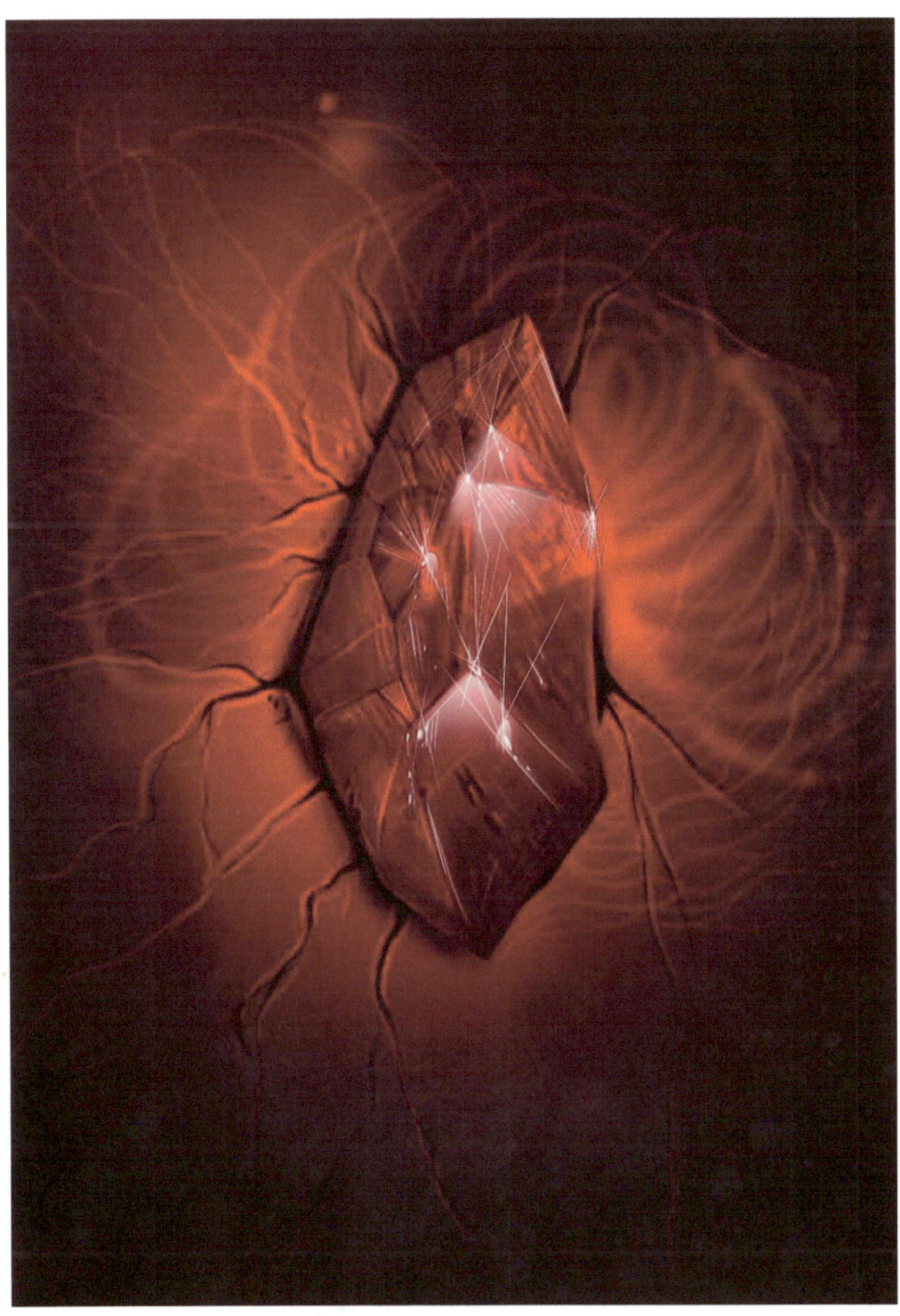

PART 4

Oscar was shot and pronounced dead. On hearing this terrible news, his father collapsed to the ground, his heart gripped by pain, and then drawing on his last remaining energy, he jumped up and said, "We have to try anyhow. We must avoid damaging the brain."

Once the electrodes were connected and the glass of the Garbmel Life capsule lowered, Nicola entered the code on the keyboard. Having no protective goggles, he closed his eyes when the lever was lowered to activate the machine. Inside, two iron blades covered with electrodes began to whirl around Oscar's lifeless body, flooding it with blue electric flashes. When the blades stopped, a hiss filled the air. Nicola opened the capsule and went to the body to check if his heart were beating, but he shook his head sorrowfully. "It's too late."

A faint voice drifted softly and broke the silence: "Dad?"

At first, Nicola thought he was dreaming. His son, still lying on the horizontal plank of the machine, was watching him.

"You're alive!"

He ran to hug him, quickly removing the electrodes and helmet from his head, then hugged him tightly though remaining silent.

He carefully moved the bandage from his stomach and then pulled it vigorously until it was completely removed. Garbmel Life had completely healed the wound.

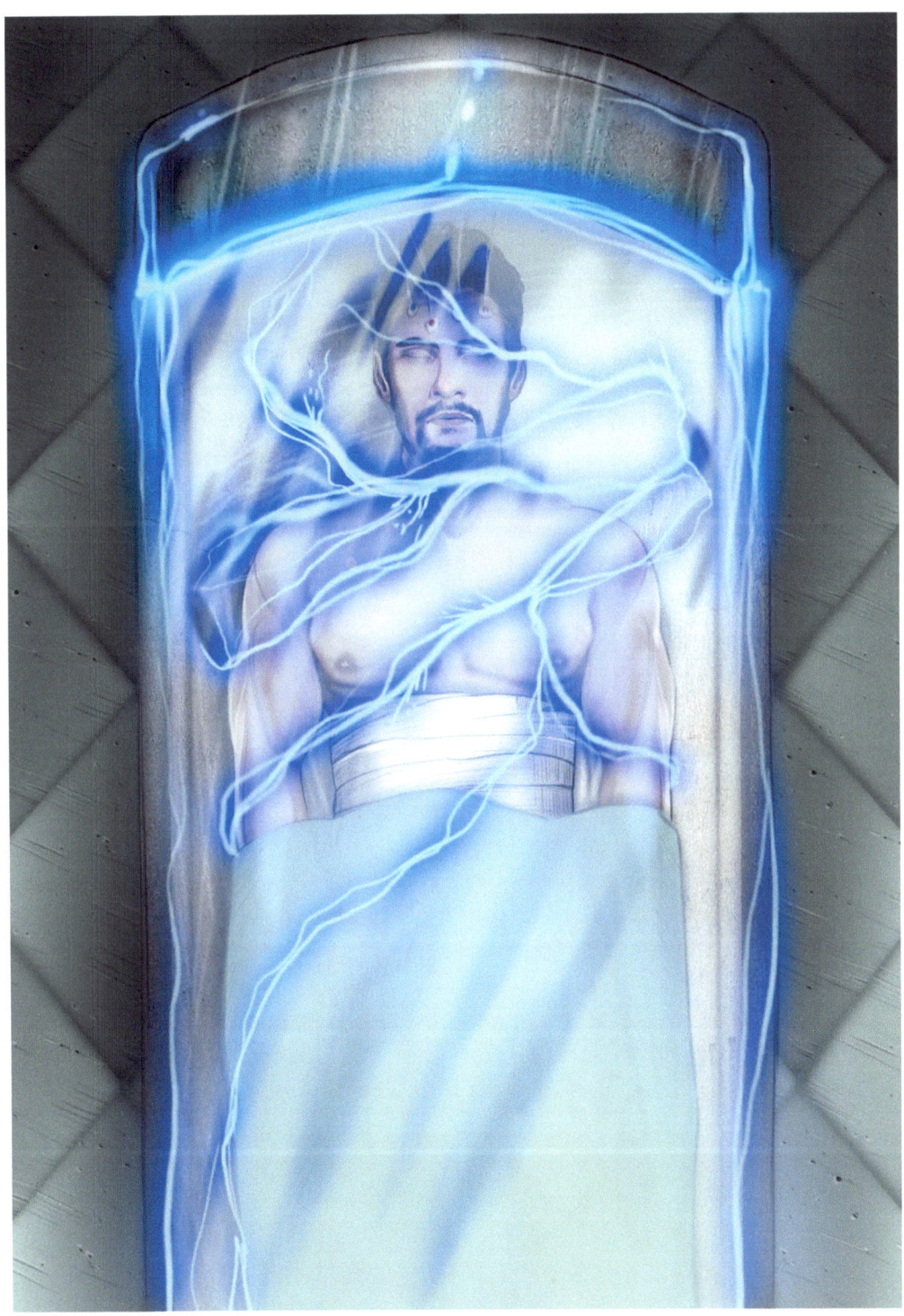

PART 5

The three went down to the basement of the villa and after going through an antechamber with a frescoed ceiling and through an armored door, they came to a large room with oblique walls. They were inside a pyramid with a vault so high that it would impress anyone who observed it. Flames from large torches lit both the walls covered with thousands of hieroglyphs and dozens of purple banners with the symbol of the snake coiled around the egg in the center. At the base of the four sides of the pyramid a number was engraved: 299.792.

The Grand Master was thinking about his father, while he solemnly advanced with his bodyguards inside the great pyramid. Many people wearing the purple dress found themselves in front of a large object covered with a cloth. As their boss went by, they lowered their heads as a sign of respect.

Two men approached the center of the room and removed the cloth from a large square-shaped machine inside which a large red stone could be glimpsed under a dusty glass plate.

He held out his hand, pointing with his index finger at the machine in the center of the room. "Using the Polemos we will send a signal to receivers that will relay it to every means of communication on earth. Anyone who is near a cell phone, a radio or any other electronic device will no longer be able to feel emotions correctly. At funerals, people will laugh, and when a child is born they will cry in sorrow! Likewise, they will feel anger towards those they love and happiness when they suffer injustice.

Right then, the elite troops of the Phanes entered the great hall marching to the beat of the drums. They paraded in front of the Grand Master, turning their faces towards him, keeping their gaze down.

PART 6

Oscar kept his hand upright enough to show his palm and instinctively pushed his thumb forward. The attacker dropped the metal tube to the ground and began to laugh as if he was in the grip of irrepressible happiness.

"I'm learning to use my powers," thought Oscar. However, the effect soon faded, the Phanes man regained control of himself, shook his head, and wondered what made him laugh like that. He reacted by hitting him with a punch in the face. Oscar fell to the ground and raised his arm again, this time stretching the little finger forward. His attacker screamed and began to punch the wall in anger. His mighty hands hit the wall until the plaster crumbled. Oscar looked at him in disbelief, he stretched his arm forward again, leaving the index finger in an advanced position. The man threw himself on the ground and with a look full of terror shouted, "They're coming! I'm scared!"

Oscar was beginning to understand how his power worked. With his hands he could manipulate the emotional state of others and, even more amazingly, every movement of the fingers was connected to a specific emotion. Although he was still stunned by the powerful blows of the attacker, he wanted to take advantage of that opportunity to once again check how his powers worked.

He stood up, standing a moment to observe the man in front of him who was still in the grip of fear. He stretched out his arm, opened the palm of his hand, and forcefully pushed his middle finger forward. The man, wrinkling his nose and lifting his upper lip, brought his hands to his face feeling a strong disgust. He ran to the window and opened it wide to breathe some fresh air, but Oscar quickly pushed his ring finger forward to elicit the expression of sadness, then his brow furrowed and the corners of his lips arched downwards. At that point, the man with the long, curled mustache knelt down, covering his face with his hands and started to cry.

Oscar instinctively joined his thumb and forefinger, immediately seeing the effects. His opponent contracted the corners of his mouth in an expression of contempt and after rolling his eyes, he remained motionless with his gaze lost in the void.

His fingers moved again, and this time he joined his thumb and little finger. The man from Phanes opened his mouth wide and pushed his eyebrows upwards, frowning: the expression of surprise was written on his face. Immediately after he began to feel a strong sense of anxiety that paralyzed him. Feeling an emotion for a fraction of a second, as often happens, has no long-term negative effect, but experiencing it continuously triggers very intense physical reactions. The Phanes hitman felt disoriented because of this whirl of emotions; the vagus nerve, one of the twelve cranial nerves, had been stimulated to such an extent by those emotional states that his blood pressure and heart rate decreased. The resulting drop in blood supply to his brain knocked him unconscious.

PART 7

When Oscar slowly opened his eyes, he realized he was lying on a cold metal gurney in a room of the Dedion. At that moment he was trying to remember what had happened when he was in Piazza Trevi before he passed out.

He tried to move his hands but found that they were secured with sturdy chains with two metal bolts. He turned his face and noticed an android clad in a white frame, more machine than human, which had emblazoned on his chest a sword symbol in the center of a golden disc topped with several gear wheels. Then he noticed Doroty, the android with the face of a woman, and circuit boards connected to her body by colored cables.

Right then, Emma and Henry entered the room through a sliding glass door, both wearing white coats and looking nervous. Emma's hair was tied up and her black eyes seemed to absorb the cold light of the neon lamps as if they were a celestial body with an intense gravitational field. No one could have deduced any details about her personality because her gaze was like a sentry with impenetrable armor. While Oscar watched Emma, he thought about how much he had missed her. Though he didn't know her well, he hadn't been able to stop thinking about her since they'd first met.

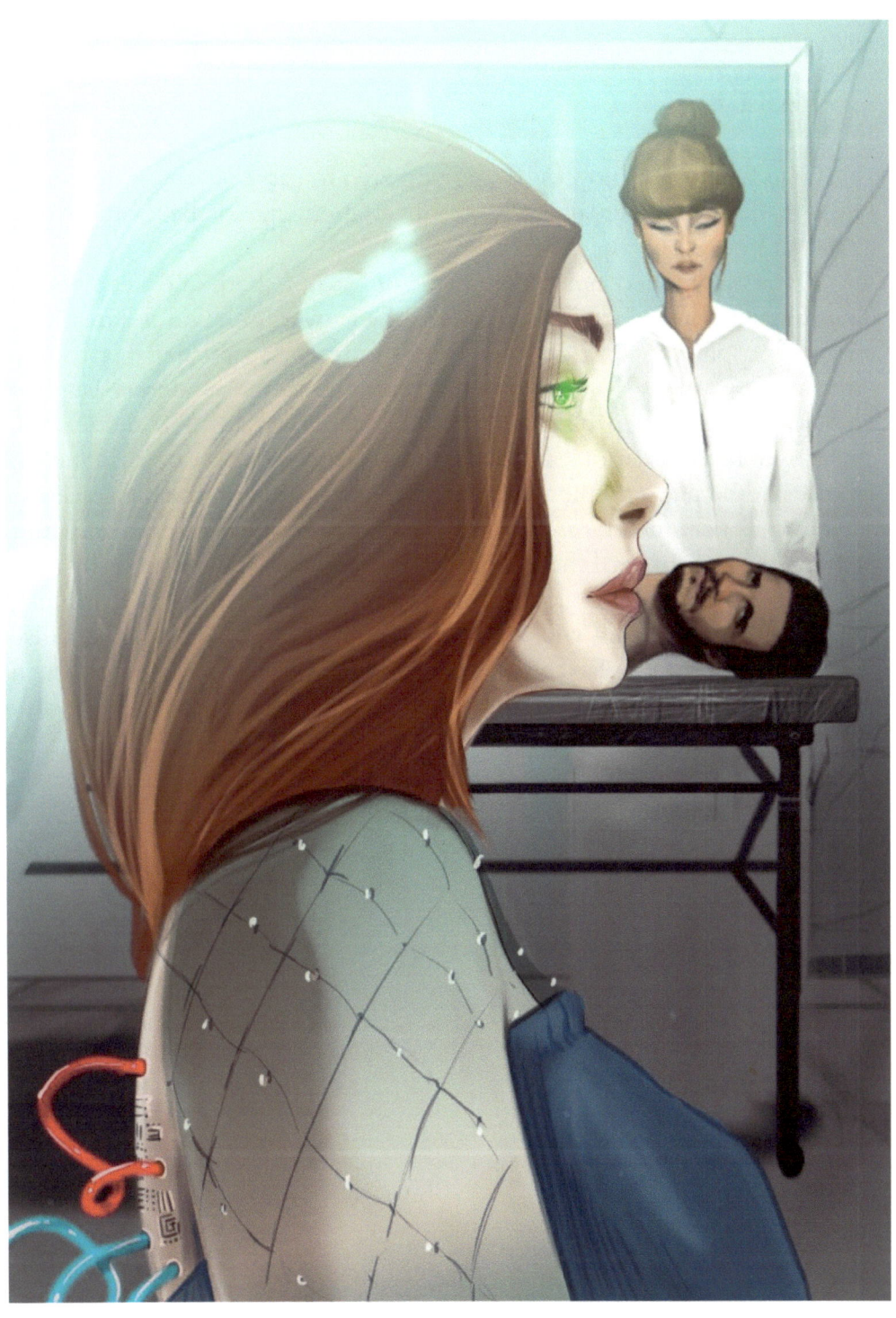

PART 8

Two Dedion employees had volunteered to carry out the experiment, though they were actually very skeptical about it, not believing in the existence of any power.

Oscar positioned himself in front of one of them and keeping his hand midair, he pushed his thumb slightly forward. Behind the man, the word "happiness" appeared on a large screen. He pushed his thumb further forward and the emotion increased until the volunteer laughed out loud. He pushed his ring finger forward and all of a sudden the employee became serious. But when he pressed his finger hard, he began to cry and behind him the word "sadness" appeared on the big screen.

Oscar positioned himself in front of the other Dedion man and after having pushed forward the index finger to stimulate the onset of fear, he did the same with the middle finger to induce the emotion of disgust, then joined the thumb and the little finger for the emotion of surprise and ended by joining his thumb and forefinger to elicit contempt. Each emotion formed on the employee's face and then led to physical manifestations.

PART 9

The underground installation had the unmistakable artistic touch of Nicola, Oscar's dad. Technologically advanced machines, albeit with an antiquated look, were everywhere; the furniture and fittings were reminiscent of Victorian style, and the rest of the installation looked like a small 19th-century town.

After ordering a security man to retrieve the driver of the van parked aboveground, Oscar and Emma entered a corridor with the ceiling partially collapsed and filled with earth. "Will this be a safe place?" Oscar thought as he entered a room full of mirrors. On the wall an old screen hung powered by a conspicuous battery dipped in a luminescent substance. A large glass bookcase held hundreds of ancient books, and a classical-style horn gramophone was playing a song in French called *La vie en rose*. Unlike the rest of the underground installation, the environment looked clean and tidy. In that atmosphere of yesteryear, a man named Cristiano wearing a long blue damask dress was intent on illustrating a parchment.

He stepped forward from the half-light and sat down on a chair; he wore a long blue damask suit with gold embroidery. Around his neck was a silver pendant, also finely decorated, from which a white light was emitted. A sword with a golden hilt was in a black scabbard fixed to his belt with silver buckles, and on the opposite hip hung an animal horn embellished with elegant inlays.

PART 10

They resumed their reconnaissance and as they were walking down a narrow alley to return to the van, a metallic clang rang out high in the sky. A man suddenly emerged from behind a dumpster and threatened them with a gun, forcing them to throw their weapons on the ground. Shortly after, at the two entrances to the alley, other men appeared in elegant but tattered clothes.

"This is the effect of the machine that changes emotions," Emma said softly. "It's called Polemos. It drove them mad and the powerful anger they felt increased their aggressiveness."

The men began to approach menacingly, brandishing iron bars and blocking any escape from the alley, but Oscar remained motionless until he could see the hate-filled eyes of the attackers.

"What should we do?" Emma asked anxiously.

"I don't understand."

"What don't you understand? We have to do something or they'll kill us!"

"When they kidnapped my father in Castel Sant'Angelo, I managed to release my power, but now something is stopping me. I'm no longer able to affect the emotions of several people at once and now have to fight them one at a time."

With a gesture of his hand made in front of the face of the man who was holding them at gunpoint, he made all forms of anger disappear. He threw the weapon to the ground looking around. "What have I done?" the man wondered incredulously a moment before he fled.

Emma picked up the gun and prepared to fire it to defend them from the imminent attack of the assailants, but the bullets inside the gun's magazine would definitely not have been enough.

Oscar told her, "Drop your weapon, we don't want to kill anyone. Stay back, your molecular suit will protect you."

He stepped forward and began to move his hands with such speed that it was difficult to even follow their path. Time and reality themselves seemed to have been altered; the attackers were moving in slow motion, while Oscar was moving at normal speed. Now his hands and fingers relentlessly moved from one side to the other and with each of his movements the facial expressions of the men changed rapidly. One of them intended to hit him with an iron bar, but he didn't even have time to lift it as expressions of happiness, anger and sadness appeared in sequence on his face. Emma could not believe her eyes and as the reality around them was moving slowly for her too, watching the scene, she could only say, "The prophecy is true, he is the star of the Perseverans... the chosen one."

PART 11

Oscar was finally able to breathe, and he imitated his opponent, Alexandros Paliesco, and he joined his hands together and started to levitate. The two went upwards spinning in the sky, facing each other with their fists out. The gravel, the marble altar itself, the braziers, as well as the tree trunks followed them towards the clouds as if sucked by the force of a hurricane and began to whirl. At that moment, they were exchanging powerful blows in the face, each followed by red and blue electric shocks. With a wave of his hand, Paliesco threw a tree trunk towards the opponent, hitting him in the chest and making him fall to the ground. Taking advantage of the opportunity, he amped up the level by throwing large rocks and the heavy marble altar against him until he was buried under it.

With a malicious grin, he landed on the grass. Aware of not being able to touch the fragment of the red stone embedded in the hollow of the molecular suit, he grabbed his bronze tool with the hook-shaped end.

Once the marble altar was removed with a simple gesture of his hand, he approached the body of the enemy who was apparently lifeless on the ground. "You wouldn't mind if I take your heart as well as the stone fragment, now would you? I'll finish what I'd left undone with your father, and Emma will die too!"

As soon as he neared the bronze tool to the opponent's chest, some metal electrical towers on the side of a road not far from there, rose and sped through the air and came down, sticking in the ground all around Oscar, creating a kind of Faraday cage. Paliesco was taken aback and jumped back to avoid them. Oscar stood up and with his eyes gleaming with light he directed his hands upwards, releasing two electric beams which rose up and came back down, striking his opponent and the area around him. The metal cage gave him protection, Paliesco could do nothing. Now he could no longer even resist the emotions that were appearing in succession on his face.

Author biography

Emiliano Forino Procacci is a psychotherapist who specializes in verbal and nonverbal communication and in encoding /decoding facial expression. After being awarded two master's degrees, he continued his training in London and California.
He has invented an innovative method for selecting personnel based on assessment techniques, reading facial micro-expressions and body language.
He is the author of several books and owner of the trademark Unstatus Luxury™.

Instagram: emiliano_forino_procacci

Facebook: Emiliano Forino Procacci

Enjoy other books by Emiliano Forino Procacci

A WORLD WITHOUT EMOTIONS (2020) – Italian and English

version.

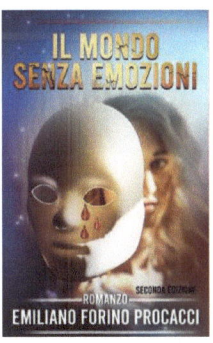

William Pattern's story begins in a world where people are no longer able to feel emotions. William is willing to go beyond all bounds to find out the truth of why things are this way. A series of twists and unexpected events lead the protagonist to encounter with an odd Resistance organization, thus discovering the importance of emotions, facial micro-expressions, and body language.

In a world filled with people with expressionless faces and ice-cold hearts comes a series of extraordinary events and an incredible love story intertwined with an action-packed plot and puzzles for the reader to solve.

A WORLD WITHOUT EMOTIONS: EVOLUTION (2020) –

Italian and English version – Third place at the Book Fest Awards

2022.

Ancient symbols and myths form the backdrop to an action-packed, twisting storyline in which William Pattern has to solve complicated puzzles to restore world order.

The protagonist goes in search of a truth buried among the monuments of a city rich in history, so that the love of truth may triumph. Guided by his instinct, he must discover what lies behind an ancient legend and mysterious Latin inscriptions.

A surreal atmosphere envelops a world in which human beings have lost their emotions and everyone wears neutral facial expressions.

This thrilling tale is the setting of a love story between two human beings made to fight for their dream of living a happy life together.

A WORLD WITHOUT EMOTIONS: THE PATH OF LIGHT (2021) – Available in Italian and soon in English.

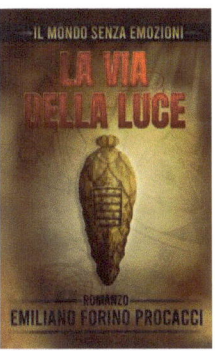

THE SUPERHERO OF EMOTION – (2022) - Available in Italian and soon in English.

A superhero, a secret organization that wants to subvert the world order and a mysterious red stone. These are just some elements of the new novel by Emiliano Forino Procacci which presents for the first time in the world an exceptional character with the ability to govern emotions.

Historical elements, action, love stories and enigmas are the background to an original plot full of twists and turns.

You can be a superhero every day by helping others, exercising willpower and calling on inner resources.

Nihil difficult volenti: nothing is difficult for the one who wants.

THE COMMUNICATION LIVES IN THE PAST - Genealogy of an ancient European family (2017) - Available in Italian and soon in English.

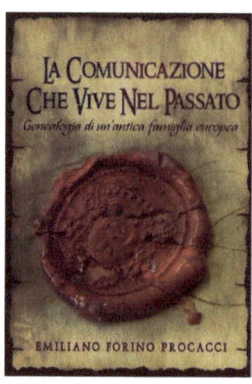

www.ingramcontent.com/pod-product-compliance
Lightning Source LLC
Chambersburg PA
CBHW042209170626
46815CB00012B/188

9 798218 009403